In
1935 if you wanted to
read a good book, you needed
either a lot of money or a library card.
Cheap paperbacks were available, but their
poor production generally mirrored the quality
between the covers. One weekend that year,
Allen Lane, Managing Director of The Bodley Head,
having spent the weekend visiting Agatha Christie,
found himself on a platform at Exeter station trying to
find something to read for his journey back to London.
He was appalled by the quality of the material he had to
choose from. Everything that Allen Lane achieved from that
day until his death in 1970 was based on a passionate belief
in the existence of 'a vast reading public for *intelligent*
books at a low price'. The result of his momentous vision
was the birth not only of Penguin, but of the 'paperback
revolution'. Quality writing became available for the price of
a packet of cigarettes, literature became a mass medium
for the first time, a nation of book-borrowers became a
nation of book-buyers – and the very concept of book
publishing was changed for ever. Those founding
principles – of quality and value, with an overarching
belief in the fundamental importance of reading –
have guided everything the company has
done since 1935. Sir Allen Lane's
pioneering spirit is still very much alive
at Penguin in 2005. Here's to
the next 70 years!

D0201562

MORE THAN A BUSINESS

'We decided it was time to end the almost customary half-hearted manner in which cheap editions were produced – as though the only people who could possibly want cheap editions must belong to a lower order of intelligence. We, however, believed in the existence in this country of a vast reading public for intelligent books at a low price, and staked everything on it'
Sir Allen Lane, 1902–1970

'The Penguin Books are splendid value for sixpence, so splendid that if other publishers had any sense they would combine against them and suppress them'
George Orwell

'More than a business ... a national cultural asset'
Guardian

'When you look at the whole Penguin achievement you know that it constitutes, in action, one of the more democratic successes of our recent social history'
Richard Hoggart

The Kiss

ANTON CHEKHOV

PENGUIN BOOKS

PENGUIN BOOKS

Published by the Penguin Group
Penguin Books Ltd, 80 Strand, London WC2R ORL, England
Penguin Group (USA) Inc., 375 Hudson Street, New York, New York 10014, USA
Penguin Group (Canada), 10 Alcorn Avenue, Toronto, Ontario, Canada M4V 3B2
(a division of Pearson Penguin Canada Inc.)
Penguin Ireland, 25 St Stephen's Green, Dublin 2, Ireland
(a division of Penguin Books Ltd)
Penguin Group (Australia), 250 Camberwell Road, Camberwell, Victoria 3124,
Australia (a division of Pearson Australia Group Pty Ltd)
Penguin Books India Pvt Ltd, 11 Community Centre,
Panchsheel Park, New Delhi – 110 017, India
Penguin Group (NZ), cnr Airborne and Rosedale Roads, Albany,
Auckland 1310, New Zealand (a division of Pearson New Zealand Ltd)
Penguin Books (South Africa) (Pty) Ltd, 24 Sturdee Avenue,
Rosebank 2196, South Africa

Penguin Books Ltd, Registered Offices: 80 Strand, London WC2R ORL, England

www.penguin.com

The Steppe and Other Stories first published in Penguin Books 2001
The Lady with the Little Dog and Other Stories first published in
Penguin Books 2002
This selection first published as a Pocket Penguin 2005

1

Translations copyright © Ronald Wilks, 1982, 1986
All rights reserved

Set in 11/13pt Monotype Dante
Typeset by Palimpsest Book Production Limited
Polmont, Stirlingshire
Printed in England by Clays Ltd, St Ives plc

Contents

The Kiss

On 20 May, at eight o'clock in the evening, all six batteries of a reserve artillery brigade, on their way back to headquarters, stopped for the night at the village of Mestechki. At the height of all the confusion – some officers were busy with the guns, while others had assembled in the main square by the churchyard fence to receive their billetings – someone in civilian dress rode up from behind the church on a strange horse: it was small and dun-coloured with a fine neck and short tail, and seemed to move sideways instead of straight ahead, making small dancing movements with its legs as if they were being whipped. When the rider came up to the officers he doffed his hat and said, 'Our squire, His Excellency, Lieutenant-General von Rabbeck, invites you for tea and would like you to come now . . .'

The horse performed a bow and a little dance, and retreated with the same sideways motion. The rider raised his hat again and quickly disappeared behind the church on his peculiar horse.

'To hell with it!' some of the officers grumbled as they rode off to their quarters. 'We want to sleep and up pops this von Rabbeck with his tea! We know what *that* means all right!'

Every officer in the six batteries vividly remembered

the previous year when they were on manoeuvres with officers from a Cossack regiment and had received a similar invitation from a landowning count, who was a retired officer. This hospitable and genial count had plied them with food and drink, would not hear of them returning to their billets and made them stay the night. That was all very well, of course, and they could not have hoped for better. But the trouble was that this retired officer was overjoyed beyond measure at having young men as his guests and he regaled them with stories from his glorious past until dawn, led them on a tour of the house, showed them his valuable paint- ings, old engravings and rare guns, and read out signed letters from eminent personages; and all this time the tired and weary officers listened, looked, pined for bed, and continuously yawned in their sleeves. When their host finally let them go, it was too late for bed.

Now, was this von Rabbeck one of the same breed? Whether he was or not, there was nothing they could do about it. The officers put clean uniforms on, smartened themselves up and went off en masse to look for the squire's house. On the square by the church they were told that they could either take the lower path leading down to the river behind the church, and then go along the bank to the garden, or they could ride direct from the church along the higher road which would bring them to the count's barns about a quarter of a mile from the village. The officers decided on the higher route.

'Who is this von Rabbeck?' they argued as they rode

along. 'Is he the one who commanded a cavalry division at Plevna?'

'No, that wasn't von Rabbeck, just Rabbe, and without the "von".'

'It's marvellous weather, anyway!'

The road divided when they reached the first barn: one fork led straight on and disappeared in the darkness of the evening, while the other turned towards the squire's house on the right. The officers took the right fork and began to lower their voices . . . Stone barns with red tiled roofs stood on both sides of the road and they had the heavy, forbidding look of some provincial barracks. Ahead of them were the lighted windows of the manor-house.

'That's a good sign, gentlemen!' one of the officers said. 'Our setter's going on in front. That means he scents game!'

Lieutenant Lobytko, a tall, strongly built officer, who was riding ahead of the others, who had no moustache (although he was over twenty-five there wasn't a trace of hair on his face), and who was renowned in the brigade for his keen senses and ability to sniff a woman out from miles away, turned round and said, 'Yes, there must be women here, my instinct tells me.'

The officers were met at the front door by von Rabbeck himself – a fine-looking man of about sixty, wearing civilian clothes. He said how very pleased and happy he was to see the officers as he shook hands, but begged them most sincerely, in the name of God, to excuse him for not inviting them to stay the night, as two sisters with their children, his brothers and some neighbours had turned up, and he didn't have one spare room.

The general shook everyone's hand, apologized and smiled, but they could tell from his face that he wasn't nearly as pleased to have guests as last year's count and he had only asked them as it was the done thing. And, as they climbed the softly carpeted stairs and listened, the officers sensed that they had been invited only because it would have caused embarrassment if they had *not* been invited. At the sight of footmen dashing around lighting the lamps in the hall and upstairs, they felt they had introduced a note of uneasiness and anxiety into the house. And how could any host be pleased at having nineteen strange officers descend on a house where two sisters, children, brothers and neighbours had already arrived, most probably to celebrate some family anniversary. They were met in the ballroom upstairs by a tall, stately old lady with black eyebrows and a long face – the living image of Empress Eugénie. She gave them a majestic, welcoming smile and said how glad and happy she was to have them as guests and apologized for the fact that she and her husband weren't able to invite the officers to stay overnight on this occasion. Her beautiful, majestic smile, which momentarily disappeared every time she turned away from her guests, revealed that in her day she had seen many officers, that she had no time for them now, and that she had invited them and was apologizing only because her upbringing and social position demanded it.

The officers entered the large dining-room where about ten gentlemen and ladies, old and young, were sitting along one side of the table having tea. Behind their chairs, enveloped in a thin haze of cigar smoke, was a group of men with a rather lean, young, red-whiskered man in the middle, rolling his 'r's as he spoke out loud in English. Behind them, through a door, was a bright room with light blue furniture.

'Gentlemen, there's so many of you, it's impossible to introduce *everyone*!' the general was saying in a loud voice, trying to sound cheerful. 'So don't stand on ceremony, introduce yourselves!'

Some officers wore very serious, even solemn expressions; others forced a smile, and all of them felt awkward as they bowed rather indifferently and sat down to tea.

Staff-Captain Ryabovich, a short, stooping officer, with spectacles and lynx-like side whiskers, was more embarrassed than anyone else. While his fellow-officers were trying to look serious or force a smile, his face, lynx-like whiskers and spectacles seemed to be saying, 'I'm the shyest, most modest and most insignificant officer in the whole brigade!' When he first entered the dining-room and sat down to tea, he found it impossible to concentrate on any one face or object. All those faces, dresses, cut-glass decanters, steaming glasses, moulded cornices, merged into one composite sensation, making Ryabovich feel ill at ease, and he longed to bury his head somewhere. Like a lecturer at his first appearance in public, he could see everything in front of him well enough, but at the same time he could make little sense of it (physicians call this condition, when someone sees without understanding, 'psychic blindness'). But after a little while Ryabovich began to feel more at home, recovered his normal vision and began to take stock of his surroundings. Since he was a timid and unsociable person, he was struck above all by what he himself had never possessed – the extra-ordinary boldness of these unfamiliar people. Von Rabbeck, two elderly ladies, a young girl in a lilac dress, and the young man with red whiskers – Rabbeck's youngest son – had sat themselves very cunningly among the officers, as though it had all been rehearsed. Straight away they had launched into a heated argu-ment, which the guests could not help joining. The girl in lilac very excitedly insisted that the artillery had a much easier time than either the cavalry or the infantry, while Rabbeck and the elderly ladies argued the contrary. A rapid conversational crossfire ensued. Ryabovich glanced at the lilac girl who was arguing so passionately about something that was so foreign to her, so utterly boring, and he could see artificial smiles flickering over her face.

Von Rabbeck and family skilfully drew the officers into the argument, at the same time watching their wine glasses with eagle eyes to check whether they were filled, that they had enough sugar, and one officer who wasn't eating biscuits or drinking any brandy worried them. The more Ryabovich looked and listened, the more he began to like this insincere but wonderfully disciplined family.

After tea the officers went into the ballroom. Lieutenant Lobytko's instinct had not failed him: the room was full of girls and young married women. Already this 'setter' lieutenant had positioned himself next to a young blonde in a black dress, bending over dashingly as though leaning on some invisible sabre, smiling and flirting with his shoulders. Most probably he was telling her some intriguing nonsense as the blonde glanced superciliously at his well-fed face and said, 'Really?'

If that 'setter' had had any brains, that cool 'Really?' should have told him that he would never be called 'to heel'.

The grand piano suddenly thundered out. The sounds of a sad waltz drifted through the wide-open windows and everyone remembered that outside it was spring, an evening in May, and they smelt the fragrance of the young leaves of the poplars, of roses and lilac. Ryabovich, feeling the effects of the brandy and the music, squinted at a window, smiled and watched the movements of the women. Now it seemed that the fragrance of the roses, the poplars and lilac wasn't coming from the garden but from the ladies' faces and dresses.

Rabbeck's son had invited a skinny girl to dance and waltzed twice round the room with her. Lobytko glided over the parquet floor as he flew up to the girl in lilac and whirled her round the room. They all began to dance . . . Ryabovich stood by the door with guests who were not dancing and watched. Not once in his life had he danced, not once had he put his arm round an attractive young woman's waist. He would usually be absolutely delighted when, with everyone looking on, a man took a young girl he hadn't met before by the waist and offered his shoulders for her to rest her hands on, but he could never imagine himself in that situation. There had been times when he envied his fellow-officers' daring and dashing ways and it made him very depressed. The realization that he was shy, round-shouldered, quite undistinguished, that he had a long waist, lynx-like side whiskers, hurt him deeply. But over the years this realization had become something of a habit and as he watched his friends dance or talk out loud he no longer envied them but was filled with sadness.

When the quadrille began, young von Rabbeck went over to the officers who were not dancing and invited two of them to a game of billiards. They accepted and left the great hall with him. As he had nothing else to do, and feeling he would like to take at least some part in what was going on, Ryabovich trudged off after them. First they went into the drawing-room, then down a narrow corridor with a glass ceiling, then into a room where three sleepy footmen leapt up from a sofa the moment they entered. Finally, after passing through a whole series of rooms, young Rabbeck and company reached a small billiard-room and the game began.

Ryabovich, who never played any games except cards, stood by the table and indifferently watched the players, cue in hand, walking up and down in their un-buttoned tunics, making puns and shouting things he could not understand. The players ignored him, only turning round to say, 'I beg your pardon', when one of them happened accidentally to nudge him with an elbow or prod him with a cue. Even before the first game was over, he was bored and began to feel he was not wanted, that he was in the way . . . He felt drawn back to the ballroom and walked away.

As he walked back he had a little adventure. Halfway, he realized he was lost – he knew very well he had to go by those three sleepy footmen, but already he had passed through five or six rooms and those footmen seemed to have vanished into thin air. He realized his mistake, retraced his steps a little and turned to the right, only to find himself in a small, dimly lit room he had not seen on the way to the billiard-room. He stood still for a minute or so, opened the first door he came to with determination and entered a completely dark room. Ahead of him he could see light coming through a crack in the door and beyond was the muffled sound of a sad mazurka. The windows here had been left open as they had in the ballroom and he could smell poplars, lilac and roses . . .

Ryabovich stopped, undecided what to do . . . Just then he was astonished to hear hurried footsteps, the rustle of a dress and a female voice whispering breathlessly, 'At last!' Two soft, sweet-smelling arms (undoubtedly a woman's) encircled his neck, a burning cheek pressed against his and at the same time there was the sound of a kiss. But immediately after the kiss the woman gave a faint cry and shrank backwards in disgust – that was how it seemed to Ryabovich.

He was on the point of crying out too and he rushed towards the bright chink in the door.

His heart pounded away when he was back in the hall and his hands trembled so obviously that he hastily hid them behind his back. At first he was tormented by shame and he feared everyone there knew he had just been embraced and kissed, and this made him hesitate and look around anxiously. But when he had convinced himself that everyone was dancing and gossiping just as peacefully as before, he gave himself up to a totally new kind of sensation, one he had never experienced before in all his life. Something strange was happening to him . . . his neck, which just a few moments ago had been embraced by sweet-smelling hands, seemed anointed with oil. And on his left cheek, just by his moustache, there was a faint, pleasant, cold, tingling sensation, the kind you get from peppermint drops and the more he rubbed the spot the stronger the tingling became. From head to heels he was overcome by a strange, new feeling which grew stronger every minute. He wanted to dance, speak to everyone, run out into the garden, laugh out loud. He completely forgot his stoop, his insignificant appearance, his lynx-like whiskers and 'vague appearance' (once he happened to hear some ladies saying this about him). When Rabbeck's wife went by he gave her such a broad, warm smile that she stopped and gave him a very searching look.

'I love this house so much!' he said, adjusting his spectacles.

The general's wife smiled and told him that the house

still belonged to her father. Then she asked if his parents were still alive, how long he had been in the army, why he was so thin, and so on . . . When Ryabovich had replied, she moved on, leaving him smiling even more warmly and he began to think he was surrounded by the most wonderful people . . .

Mechanically, Ryabovich ate and drank everything he was offered at the dinner table, deaf to everything as he tried to find an explanation for what had just happened. It was a mysterious, romantic incident, but it wasn't difficult to explain. No doubt some girl or young married woman had a rendezvous with someone in that dark room, had waited for a long time, and then mistook Ryabovich for her hero in her nervous excitement. This was the most likely explanation, all the more so as Ryabovich had hesitated in the middle of the room, which made it look as though he were expecting someone . . .

'But who *is* she?' he thought as he surveyed the ladies' faces. 'She must be young, as old ladies don't have rendezvous. And intelligent – I could tell from the rustle of her dress, her smell, her voice.'

He stared at the girl in lilac and found her very attractive. She had beautiful shoulders and arms, a clever face and a fine voice. As he gazed at her, Ryabovich wanted *her*, no one else, to be that mysterious stranger . . . But she gave a rather artificial laugh and wrinkled her long nose, which made her look old. Then he turned to the blonde in black. She was younger, simpler and less affected, with charming temples and she sipped daintily from her wine glass. Now Ryabovich wanted her to be the stranger. But he soon discovered that she had a featureless face and he turned to her neighbour . . . 'It's hard to say,' he wondered dreamily. 'If I could just take the lilac girl's shoulders and arms away, add the blonde's temples, then take those eyes away from the girl on Lobytko's left, *then*.' He merged them all into one, so that he had an image of the girl who had kissed him, the image he desired so much, but which he just could not find among the guests around the table.

After dinner the officers, well-fed and slightly tipsy by now, began to make their farewells and expressed their thanks. Once again the hosts apologized for not having them stay the night.

'Delighted, gentlemen, absolutely delighted,' the general was saying and this time he meant it – probably because people are usually more sincere and better-humoured saying goodbye to guests than welcoming them.

'Delighted! Glad to see you back any time, so don't stand on ceremony. Which way are you going? The higher road? No, go through the garden, it's quicker.'

The officers went into the garden, where it seemed very dark and quiet after the bright lights and the noise. They did not say a word all the way to the gate. They were half-drunk, cheerful and contented, but the darkness and the silence made them pause for thought. Probably they were thinking the same as Ryabovich: would they ever see the day when they would own a large house, have a family, a garden, when *they* too would be able to entertain people (however much of a pretence this might be), feed them well, make them drunk and happy?

As they went through the garden gate they all started talking at once and, for no apparent reason, laughed out loud. Now they were descending the path that led down to the river and then ran along the water's edge, weaving its way around the bushes, the little pools of water and the willows which overhung the river. The bank and the path were barely visible, and the far side was plunged in darkness. Here and there were reflections of the stars in the water, quivering and breaking up into little patches – the only sign that the river was flowing fast. All was quiet. Sleepy sandpipers called plaintively from the far bank and on the near side a nightingale in a bush poured out its song, ignoring the passing officers.

The men paused by the bush, touched it, but still the nightingale sang.

'That's a bird for you!' approving voices murmured. 'Here we are, right next to him and he doesn't take a blind bit of notice! What a rascal!'

The path finally turned upwards and came out on to the high road by the church fence. The officers were exhausted from walking up the hill and sat down for a smoke. On the far bank they could make out a dim red light and they tried to pass the time by guessing whether it was a camp fire, a light in a window, or something else . . . Ryabovich looked at it and imagined that the light was winking at him and smiling, as though it knew all about that kiss.

When he reached his quarters Ryabovich quickly undressed and lay on his bed. In the same hut were Lobytko and Lieutenant Merzlyakov, a gentle, rather quiet young man, who was considered well-educated in his own little circle. He was always reading the *European Herald* when he had the chance and took it with him everywhere. Lobytko undressed, paced up and down for a long time, with the expression of a dissatisfied man, and sent the batman for some beer.

Merzlyakov lay down, placed a candle near his pillow and immersed himself in the *European Herald*.

'Who *is* she?' Ryabovich wondered as he glanced at the grimy ceiling. His neck still felt as if it had been anointed with oil and he had that tingling sensation around his mouth – just like peppermint drops. He had fleeting visions of the lilac girl's shoulders and arms, the temples and truthful eyes of the blonde in black, waists, dresses, brooches. He tried to fix these visions firmly in his mind, but they kept dancing about, dissolving, flickering. When these visions vanished completely against that darkened background everyone has when he closes his eyes, he began to hear hurried steps, rustling dresses, the sound of a kiss and he was gripped by an inexplicable, overwhelming feeling of joy. Just as he was abandoning himself to it, he heard the batman come back and report that there wasn't any beer. Lobytko became terribly agitated and started pacing up and down again.

'Didn't I tell you he's an idiot?' he said, stopping first in front of Ryabovich, then Merzlyakov. 'A man must really be a blockhead and idiot to come back without any beer! The man's a rogue, eh?'

'Of course, you won't find any beer in this place,' Merzlyakov said without taking his eyes off the *European Herald*.

'Oh, do you really think so?' Lobytko persisted. 'Good God, put me on the moon and I'll find you beer and women right away! Yes, I'll go now and find some . . . Call me a scoundrel if I don't succeed!'

He slowly dressed and pulled on his high boots. Then he finished his cigarette in silence and left.

'Rabbeck, Grabbeck, Labbeck,' he muttered, pausing in the hall. 'I don't feel like going on my own, dammit! Fancy a little walk, Ryabovich?'

There was no reply, so he came back, slowly undressed and got into bed. Merzlyakov sighed, put the *European Herald* away and snuffed the candle.

'Hm,' Lobytko murmured as he puffed his cigarette in the dark.

Ryabovich pulled the blankets over his head, curled himself into a ball and tried to merge the visions fleeting through his mind into one fixed image. But he failed completely. Soon he fell asleep and his last waking thought was of someone caressing him and making him happy, of something absurd and unusual, but nonetheless exceptionally fine and joyful, that had entered his life. And his dreams centred around this one thought.

When he woke up, the sensation of oil on his cheek and the minty tingling near his lips had vanished, but the joy of yesterday still filled his heart. Delighted, he watched the window frames, gilded now by the rising sun, and listened intently to the street noises. Outside, just by the window, he could hear loud voices – Lebedetsky, Ryabovich's battery commander, who had just caught up with the brigade, was shouting at his sergeant – simply because he had lost the habit of talking softly.

'Is there anything else?' he roared.

'When they were shoeing yesterday, sir, someone drove a nail into Pigeon's hoof. The medical orderly put clay and vinegar on it and they're keeping the horse reined, away from the others. And artificer Artemyev got drunk yesterday and the lieutenant had him tied to the fore-carriage of an auxiliary field-gun.'

And the sergeant had more to report. Karpov had forgotten the new cords for the trumpets and the stakes for the tents, and the officers had spent the previous evening as guests of General von Rabbeck. During the conversation, Lebedetsky's head and red beard appeared at the window. He blinked his short-sighted eyes at the sleepy officers and bade them good morning.

'Everything all right?' he asked.

'One of the shaft-horses damaged its withers – it was the new collar,' Lobytko answered, yawning.

The commander sighed, pondered for a moment and said in a loud voice, 'I'm still wondering whether to pay Aleksandra a visit, I really ought to go and see how she is. Well, goodbye for now, I'll catch you up by evening.'

A quarter of an hour later the brigade moved off. As it passed the general's barns, Ryabovich looked to the right where the house was. The blinds were drawn in all the windows. Clearly, everyone was still asleep. And the girl who had kissed Ryabovich the day before was sleeping too. He tried to imagine her as she slept and he had a clear and distinct picture of the wide-open windows, the little green branches peeping into her bedroom, the morning freshness, the smell of poplars, lilac and roses, her bed and the chair with that dress which had rustled the day before lying over it, tiny slippers, a watch on the table. But the actual features of that face, that sweet, dreamy smile, exactly what was most characteristic of her, slipped through his imagination like mercury through the fingers. When he had ridden about a quarter of a mile, he looked back. The yellow church, the house, the river and garden were flooded in sunlight and the river, with its bright green banks and its waters reflecting the light blue sky and glinting silver here and there, looked very beautiful. Ryabovich took a last look at Mestechki and he felt so sad, as if he were saying farewell to what was very near and dear to him.

But there were only long-familiar, boring scenes ahead of him. On both sides of the road there were fields of young rye and buckwheat, where crows were hopping about. Ahead, all he could see was dust and the backs of soldiers' heads; and behind, the same dust, the same faces. The brigade was led by a vanguard of four soldiers bearing sabres and behind them rode the military choristers, followed by trumpeters. Every now and then, like torchbearers in a funeral cortège, the vanguard and singers ignored the regulation distance and pushed on far ahead. Ryabovich rode alongside the first field-gun of the fifth battery and he could see the other four in front. These long, ponderous processions formed by brigades on the move can strike civilians as very peculiar, an unintelligible muddle, and non-military people just cannot fathom why a single field-gun has to be escorted by so many soldiers, why it has to be drawn by so many horses all tangled up in such strange harness, as if it really was such a terrible, heavy object. But Ryabovich understood everything perfectly well and for that reason he found it all extremely boring. He had long known why a hefty bombardier always rides with the officer at the head of every battery and why he is called an outrider. Immediately behind this bombardier came the riders on the first, then the middle-section trace-horses. Ryabovich knew that the horses to the left were saddle-horses, while those on the right were auxiliary – all this was very boring. The horsemen were followed by two shaft-horses, one ridden by a horseman with yesterday's dust still on his back and who had a clumsy-looking, very comical piece of wood fixed to his right leg. Ryabovich knew what it was for and did not find it funny. All the riders waved their whips mechanically and shouted now and again. As for the field-gun, it was an ugly thing. Sacks of oats covered with tarpaulin lay on the fore-carriage and the gun itself was hung with kettles, kitbags and little sacks: it resembled a small harmless animal which had been surrounded, for some reason, by men and horses. On the side sheltered from the wind a team of six strode along, swinging their arms. This gun was followed by more bombardiers, riders, shaft-horses and another field-gun – just as ugly and uninspiring as the first – lumbering along in the rear. After the second gun came a third, then a fourth with an officer riding alongside (there are six batteries to a brigade and four guns to a battery). The whole procession stretched about a quarter of a mile and ended with the baggage wagons, where a most likeable creature plodded thoughtfully along, his long-eared head drooping: this was Magar the donkey, brought from Turkey by a certain battery commander.

Ryabovich looked apathetically at all those necks and faces in front and behind. At any other time he would have dozed off, but now he was immersed in new, pleasant thoughts. When the brigade had first set off, he had tried to convince himself that the incident of the kiss was only some unimportant, mysterious adventure and that essentially it was trivial and too ridiculous for serious thought. But very quickly he waved logic aside and gave himself up to his dreams. First he pictured himself in von Rabbeck's drawing-room, sitting next to a girl who resembled both the girl in lilac and the blonde in black. Then he closed his eyes and imagined himself with another, completely strange girl, with very indeterminate features: in his thoughts he spoke to her, caressed her and leaned his head on her shoulder. Then he thought of war and separation, reunion, dinner with his wife and children . . .

'Brakes on!' rang out the command every time they

went downhill. He shouted the command too, and feared that his own shouts would shatter his daydreams and bring him back to reality.

As they passed some estate, Ryabovich peeped over the fence into the garden. There he saw a long avenue, straight as a ruler, strewn with yellow sand and lined with young birches. With the eagerness of a man who has surrendered himself to daydreaming, he imagined tiny female feet walking over the yellow sand. And, quite unexpectedly, he had a clear mental picture of the girl who had kissed him, the girl he had visualized the previous evening during dinner. This image had planted itself in his mind and would not leave him.

At midday someone shouted from a wagon in the rear, 'Attention, eyes left! Officers!'

The brigadier drove up in an open carriage drawn by two white horses. He ordered it to stop near the second battery and shouted something no one understood. Several officers galloped over to him, Ryabovich among them.

'Well, what's the news?' asked the brigadier, blinking his red eyes. 'Anyone ill?'

When they had replied, the brigadier, a small skinny man, chewed for a moment, pondered and then turned to one of the officers: 'One of your drivers, on the third gun, has taken his knee-guard off and the devil's hung it on the fore-carriage. Reprimand him!'

He looked up at Ryabovich and continued: 'It strikes me your harness breeches are too long.'

After a few more tiresome comments, the brigadier

glanced at Lobytko and grinned. 'You look down in the dumps today, Lieutenant Lobytko. Pining for Madame Lopukhov, eh? Gentlemen, he's pining for Madame Lopukhov!'

Madame Lopukhov was a very plump, tall lady, well past forty. The brigadier, who had a passion for large women, no matter what age, suspected his officers nurtured similar passions. They smiled politely. Then the brigadier, delighted with himself for having made a very amusing, cutting remark, roared with laughter, tapped his driver on the back and saluted. The carriage drove off.

'All the things I'm dreaming about now and which seem impossible, out of this world, are in fact very ordinary,' Ryabovich thought as he watched the clouds of dust rising in the wake of the brigadier's carriage. 'It's all so very ordinary, everyone experiences it . . . The brigadier, for example. He was in love once, now he's married, with children. Captain Vachter is married and loved, despite having an extremely ugly red neck and no waistline. Salmanov is coarse and too much of a Tartar, but *he* had an affair that finished in marriage. I'm the same as everyone else . . . sooner or later I'll have to go through what they did . . .'

And he was delighted and encouraged by the thought that he was just an ordinary man, leading an ordinary life. Now he was bold enough to picture *her* and his happiness as much as he liked and he gave full rein to his imagination.

In the evening, when the brigade had reached its

destination and the officers were resting in their tents, Ryabovich, Merzlyakov and Lobytko gathered round a trunk and had supper. Merzlyakov took his time, holding his *European Herald* on his knees and reading it as he slowly munched his food.

Lobytko could not stop talking and kept filling his glass with beer, while Ryabovich, whose head was rather hazy from dreaming all day long, said nothing as he drank. Three glasses made him tipsy and weak and he felt an irrepressible longing to share his new feelings with his friends.

'A strange thing happened to me at the Rabbecks,' he said, trying to sound cool and sarcastic. 'I went to the billiard-room, you know . . .'

He began to tell them, in great detail, all about the kiss, but after a minute fell silent. In that one minute he had told them everything and he was astonished when he considered how little time was needed to tell his story: he had imagined it would take until morning. After he heard the story, Lobytko – who was a great liar and therefore a great sceptic – looked at him in disbelief and grinned. Merzlyakov twitched his eyebrows and kept his eyes glued to the *European Herald* as he calmly remarked, 'Damned if I know what to make of it! Throwing herself round a stranger's neck without saying a word first . . . She must have been a mental case . . .'

'Yes, some kind of neurotic,' Ryabovich agreed.

'Something similar happened to me once,' Lobytko said, assuming a frightened look. 'Last year I was travelling to Kovno . . . second class. The compartment was chock-full and it was impossible to sleep. So I tipped the guard fifty copeks . . . he took my luggage and got me a berth in a sleeper. I lay down and covered myself with a blanket. It was dark, you understand. Suddenly someone was touching my shoulder and breathing into my face. So I moved my arm and felt an elbow. I opened my eyes and – can you imagine! – it was a woman. Black eyes, lips as red as the best salmon, nostrils breathing passion, breasts like buffers! . . .'

'Just a minute,' Merzlyakov calmly interrupted. 'I don't dispute what you said about her breasts, but how could you see her lips if it was dark?'

Lobytko tried to wriggle out by poking fun at Merzlyakov's obtuseness and this jarred on Ryabovich. He went away from the trunk, lay down and vowed never again to tell his secrets.

Camp life fell back into its normal routine. The days flashed by, each exactly the same as the other. All this time Ryabovich felt, thought and behaved like someone in love. When his batman brought him cold water in the mornings, he poured it over his head and each time he remembered that there was something beautiful and loving in his life.

In the evenings, when his fellow-officers talked about love and women, he would listen very attentively, sitting very close to them and assuming the habitual expression of a soldier hearing stories about battles he himself fought in. On those evenings when senior officers, led by 'setter' Lobytko, carried out 'sorties' on the local village, in true Don Juan style, Ryabovich went along with them and invariably returned feeling sad, deeply guilty and imploring *her* forgiveness. In his spare time, or on nights when he couldn't sleep, when he wanted to recall his childhood days, his parents, everything that was near and dear to him, he would always find himself thinking of Mestechki instead, of that strange horse, of von Rabbeck and his wife, who looked like the Empress Eugénie, of that dark room with the bright chink in the door.

On 31 August he left camp – not with his own brigade, however, but with two batteries. All the way he daydreamed and became very excited, as though he were going home. He wanted passionately to see that strange horse again, the church, those artificial Rabbecks, the dark room. Some inner voice, which so often deceives those in love, whispered that he was *bound* to see her again. And he was tormented by such questions as: how could he arrange a meeting, what would she say, had she forgotten the kiss? If the worst came to the worst, he would at least have the pleasure of walking through that dark room and remembering . . .

Towards evening, that familiar church and the white barns appeared on the horizon. His heart began to pound. He did not listen to what the officer riding next to him was saying, he was oblivious of everything and looked eagerly at the river gleaming in the distance, at the loft above which pigeons were circling in the light of the setting sun.

As he rode up to the church and heard the quartermaster speaking, he expected a messenger on horseback to appear from behind the fence any minute and invite the officers to tea . . . but the quartermaster read the billeting list out, the officers dismounted and strolled off into the village – and no messenger came.

'The people in the village will tell Rabbeck we're here and he'll send for us,' Ryabovich thought as he went into his hut. He just could not understand why a fellow-officer was lighting a candle, why the batmen were hurriedly heating the samovars.

He was gripped by an acute feeling of anxiety. He lay down, then got up and looked out of the window to see if the messenger was coming. But there was no one. He lay down again but got up again after half an hour, unable to control his anxiety, went out into the street and strode off towards the church.

The square near the fence was dark and deserted. Some soldiers were standing in a row at the top of the slope, saying nothing. They jumped when they saw Ryabovich and saluted. He acknowledged the salute and went down the familiar path.

The entire sky over the far bank was flooded with crimson; the moon was rising. Two peasant women were talking loudly and picking cabbage leaves as they walked along the edge of a kitchen garden. Beyond the gardens were some dark huts. On the near bank everything was much the same as in May: the path, the bushes, the willows overhanging the river . . . only there was no bold nightingale singing, no fragrant poplars or young grass. Ryabovich reached the garden and peered over the gate. It was dark and quiet and all he could see were the white trunks of the nearest birches and here and there little patches of avenue – everything else had merged into one black mass. Ryabovich looked hard, listened eagerly, and after standing and waiting for about a quarter of an hour, without hearing a sound or seeing a single light, he trudged wearily away . . .

He went down to the river, where he could see the general's bathing-hut and towels hanging over the rail on the little bridge. He went on to the bridge, stood for a moment and aimlessly fingered the towels. They felt cold and rough. He looked down at the water . . . the current was swift and purled, barely audibly, against the piles of the hut. The red moon was reflected in the water near the left bank; tiny waves rippled through the reflection, pulling it apart and breaking it up into little patches, as if trying to bear it away.

'How stupid, how very stupid!' Ryabovich thought as he looked at the fast-flowing water. Now, when he hoped for nothing, that adventure of the kiss, his impatience, his vague longings and disillusionment appeared in a new light. He didn't think it at all strange that he hadn't waited for the general's messenger or that he would never see the girl who had kissed him by mistake. On the contrary, he would have thought it strange if he *had* seen her . . .

The water raced past and he did not know where or why; it had flowed just as swiftly in May, when it grew from a little stream into a large river, flowed into the sea, evaporated and turned into rain. Perhaps this was the same water flowing past. To what purpose?

And the whole world, the whole of life, struck

Ryabovich as a meaningless, futile joke. As he turned his eyes from the water to the sky, he remembered how fate had accidentally caressed him – in the guise of an unknown woman. He recalled the dreams and visions of that summer and his life seemed terribly empty, miserable, colourless . . . When he returned to his hut, none of the officers was there.

The batman reported that they had all gone to 'General Fontryabkin's' – he'd sent a messenger on horseback with the invitation. There was a brief flicker of joy in his heart, but he snuffed it out at once, lay on his bed and in defiance of fate – as though he wanted to bring its wrath down on his own head – he did not go to the general's.

A Visit to Friends

(A STORY)

A letter arrived one morning.

Kuzminki, June 7th
Dear Misha,
You've completely forgotten us, please come and visit us soon,
we so want to see you. Come today. We beg you, dear sir,
on bended knees! Show us your radiant eyes!
Can't wait to see you,
Ta and Va

The letter was from Tatyana Alekseyevna Losev, who
had been called 'Ta' for short when Podgorin was staying at Kuzminki ten or twelve years ago. But who was
this 'Va'? Podgorin recalled the long conversations, the
gay laughter, the love affairs, the evening walks and that
whole array of girls and young women who had once
lived at Kuzminki and in the neighbourhood. And he
remembered that open, lively, clever face with freckles
that matched chestnut hair so well – this was Varvara
Pavlovna, Tatyana's friend. Varvara Pavlovna had taken
a degree in medicine and was working at a factory somewhere beyond Tula. Evidently she had come to stay at
Kuzminki now.

'Dear Va!' thought Podgorin, surrendering himself to memories. 'What a wonderful girl!'

Tatyana, Varvara and himself were all about the same age. But he had been a mere student then and they were already marriageable girls – in their eyes he was just a boy. And now, even though he had become a lawyer and had started to go grey, all of them still treated him like a youngster, saying that he had no experience of life yet.

He was very fond of them, but more as a pleasant memory than in actuality, it seemed. He knew little about their present life, which was strange and alien to him. And this brief, playful letter too was something quite foreign to him and had most probably been written after much time and effort. When Tatyana wrote it her husband Sergey Sergeich was doubtlessly standing behind her. She had been given Kuzminki as her dowry only six years before, but this same Sergey Sergeich had already reduced the estate to bankruptcy. Each time a bank or mortgage payment became due they would now turn to Podgorin for legal advice. Moreover, they had twice asked him to lend them money. So it was obvious that they either wanted advice or a loan from him now.

He no longer felt so attracted to Kuzminki as in the past. It was such a miserable place. That laughter and rushing around, those cheerful carefree faces, those rendezvous on quiet moonlit nights – all this had gone. Most important, though, they weren't in the flush of youth any more. Probably it enchanted him only as a memory, nothing else. Besides Ta and Va, there was someone called 'Na', Tatyana's sister Nadezhda, whom half-joking, half-seriously they had called his fiancée. He had seen her grow up and everyone expected him to marry her. He had loved her once and was going to propose. But there she was, twenty-three now, and he still hadn't married her.

'Strange it should turn out like this,' he mused as he reread the letter in embarrassment. 'But I can't *not* go, they'd be offended.'

His long absence from the Losevs lay like a heavy weight on his conscience. After pacing his room and reflecting at length, he made a great effort of will and decided to go and visit them for about three days and so discharge his duty. Then he could feel free and relaxed – at least until the following summer. After lunch, as he prepared to leave for the Brest Station, he told his servants that he would be back in three days.

It was two hours by train from Moscow to Kuzminki, then a twenty-minute carriage drive from the station, from which he could see Tatyana's wood and those three tall, narrow holiday villas that Losev (he had entered upon some business enterprise in the first years of his marriage) had started building but had never finished. He had been ruined by these holiday villas, by various business projects, by frequent trips to Moscow, where he used to lunch at the Slav Fair and dine at the Hermitage, ending up in Little Bronny Street or at a gipsy haunt named Knacker's Yard, calling this 'having a fling'. Podgorin liked a drink himself – sometimes quite a lot – and he associated with women indiscriminately, but in a cool, lethargic way, without deriving any pleasure. It sickened him when others gave themselves up to these pleasures with such zest. He didn't understand or like men who could feel more free and easy at the Knacker's Yard than at home with a respectable woman, and he felt that any kind of promiscuity stuck to them like burrs. He didn't care for Losev, considering him a boring, lazy, old bungler and more than once had found his company rather repulsive.

Just past the wood, Sergey Sergeich and Nadezhda met him.

'My dear fellow, why have you forgotten us?' Sergey Sergeich asked, kissing him three times and then putting both arms round his waist. 'You don't feel affection for us any more, old chap.'

He had coarse features, a fat nose and a thin, light-brown beard. He combed his hair to one side to make himself look like a typical simple Russian. When he spoke he breathed right into your face and when he wasn't speaking he'd breathe heavily through the nose. He was embarrassed by his plumpness and inordinately replete appearance and would keep thrusting out his chest to breathe more easily, which made him look pompous.

In comparison, his sister-in-law Nadezhda seemed ethereal. She was very fair, pale-faced and slim, with kind, loving eyes. Podgorin couldn't judge as to her beauty, since he'd known her since she was a child and grown used to the way she looked. Now she was wearing a white, open-necked dress and the sight of that long, white bare neck was new to him and not altogether pleasant.

'My sister and I have been waiting for you since morning,' she said. 'Varvara's here and she's been expecting you, too.'

She took his arm and suddenly laughed for no reason, uttering a faint cry of joy as if some thought had unexpectedly cast a spell over her. The fields of flowering rye, motionless in the quiet air, the sunlit wood – they were so beautiful. Nadezhda seemed to notice these things only now, as she walked at Podgorin's side.

'I'll be staying about three days,' he told her. 'I'm sorry, but I just couldn't get away from Moscow any earlier.'

'That's not very nice at all, you've forgotten we exist!' Sergey Sergeich said, reproaching him good-humouredly. '*Jamais de ma vie!*' he suddenly added, snapping his fingers. He had this habit of suddenly blurting out some irrelevance, snapping his fingers in the process. He was always mimicking someone: if he rolled his eyes, or nonchalantly tossed his hair back, or adopted a dramatic pose, that meant he had been to the theatre the night before, or to some dinner with speeches. Now he took short steps as he walked, like an old gout-ridden man, and without bending his knees – he was most likely imitating someone.

'Do you know, Tanya wouldn't believe you'd come,' Nadezhda said. 'But Varvara and I had a funny feeling about it. I somehow *knew* you'd be on that train.'

'*Jamais de ma vie!*' Sergey Sergeich repeated.

The ladies were waiting for them on the garden terrace. Ten years ago Podgorin – then a poor student – had given Nadezhda coaching in maths and history in exchange for board and lodging. Varvara, who was studying medicine at the time, happened to be taking Latin lessons from him. As for Tatyana, already a beautiful mature girl then, she could think of nothing but love. All she had desired was love and happiness and she would yearn for them, forever waiting for the husband she dreamed of night and day. Past thirty now, she was just as beautiful and attractive as ever, in her loose-fitting peignoir and with those plump, white arms. Her only thought was for her husband and two little girls. Although she was talking and smiling now, her expression revealed that she was preoccupied with other matters. She was still guarding her love and her rights to that love and was always on the alert, ready to attack any enemy who might want to take her husband and children away from her. Her love was very strong and she felt that it was reciprocated, but jealousy and fear for her children were a constant torment and prevented her from being happy.

After the noisy reunion on the terrace, everyone except Sergey Sergeich went to Tatyana's room. The sun's rays did not penetrate the lowered blinds and it was so gloomy there that all the roses in a large bunch looked the same colour. They made Podgorin sit down in an old armchair by the window; Nadezhda sat on a low stool at his feet. Besides the kindly reproaches, the jokes and laughter that reminded him so clearly of the past, he knew he could expect an unpleasant conversation about promissory notes and mortgages. It couldn't be avoided, so he thought that it might be best to get down to business there and then without delaying matters, to get it over and done with and then go out into the garden, into fresh air.

'Shall we discuss business first?' he said. 'What's new here in Kuzminki? Is something rotten in the state of Denmark?'

'Kuzminki is in a bad way,' Tatyana replied, sadly sighing. 'Things are so bad it's hard to imagine they could be any worse.' She paced the room, highly agitated. 'Our estate's for sale, the auction's on 7 August. Everywhere there's advertisements, and buyers come here – they walk through the house, looking . . . Now anyone has the right to go into my room and look round. That may be legal, but it's humiliating for me and deeply insulting. We've no funds – and there's nowhere left to borrow any from. Briefly, it's shocking!'

She stopped in the middle of the room, the tears trickling from her eyes, and her voice trembled as she went on, 'I swear, I swear by all that's holy, by my children's happiness, I can't live without Kuzminki! I was born here, it's my home. If they take it away from me I shall never get over it, I'll die of despair.'

'I think you're rather looking on the black side,' Podgorin said. 'Everything will turn out all right. Your husband will get a job, you'll settle down again, lead a new life . . .'

'How *can* you say that!' Tatyana shouted. Now she

looked very beautiful and aggressive. She was ready to fall on the enemy who wanted to take her husband, children and home away from her, and this was expressed with particular intensity in her face and whole figure. 'A new life! I ask you! Sergey Sergeich's been busy applying for jobs and they've promised him a position as tax inspector somewhere near Ufa or Perm – or thereabouts. I'm ready to go anywhere. Siberia even. I'm prepared to live there ten, twenty years, but I must be certain that sooner or later I'll return to Kuzminki. I can't live without Kuzminki. I can't, and I won't!' She shouted and stamped her foot.

'Misha, you're a lawyer,' Varvara said, 'you know all the tricks and it's your job to advise us what to do.'

There was only one fair and reasonable answer to this, that there was nothing anyone could do, but Podgorin could not bring himself to say it outright.

'I'll . . . have a think about it,' he mumbled indecisively. 'I'll have a think about it . . .'

He was really two different persons. As a lawyer he had to deal with some very ugly cases. In court and with clients he behaved arrogantly and always expressed his opinion bluntly and curtly. He was used to crudely living it up with his friends. But in his private, intimate life he displayed uncommon tact with people close to him or with very old friends. He was shy and sensitive and tended to beat about the bush. One tear, one sidelong glance, a lie or even a rude gesture was enough to make him wince and lose his nerve. Now that Nadezhda was sitting at his feet he disliked her bare neck. It palled on him and even made him feel like going home. A year ago he had happened to bump into Sergey Sergeich at a certain Madame's place in Little Bronny Street and he now felt awkward in Tatyana's company, as if *he* had been the unfaithful one. And this conversation about Kuzminki put him in the most dreadful difficulties. He was used to having ticklish, unpleasant questions decided by judge or jury, or by some legal clause, but faced with a problem that he personally had to solve he was all at sea.

'You're our friend, Misha. We all love you as if you were one of the family,' Tatyana continued. 'And I'll tell you quite candidly: all our hopes rest in you. For heaven's sake, tell us what to do. Perhaps we could write somewhere for help? Perhaps it's not too late to put the estate in Nadezhda's or Varvara's name? What shall we do?'

'Please save us, Misha, *please*,' Varvara said, lighting a cigarette. 'You were always so clever. You haven't seen much of life, you're not very experienced, but you have a fine brain. You'll help Tatyana. I know you will.'

'I must think about it . . . perhaps I can come up with something.'

They went for a walk in the garden, then in the fields. Sergey Sergeich went too. He took Podgorin's arm and led him on ahead of the others, evidently intending to discuss something with him – probably the trouble he was in. Walking with Sergey Sergeich and talking to him were an ordeal too. He kept kissing him – always three kisses at a time – took

Podgorin's arm, put his own arm round his waist and breathed into his face. He seemed covered with sweet glue that would stick to you if he came close. And that look in his eyes which showed that he wanted something from Podgorin, that he was about to ask him for it, was really quite distressing – it was like having a revolver aimed at you.

The sun had set and it was growing dark. Green and red lights appeared here and there along the railway line. Varvara stopped and as she looked at the lights she started reciting:

> The line runs straight, unswerving,
> Through narrow cuttings,
> Passing posts, crossing bridges,
> While all along the verges,
> Lie buried so many Russian workers!

'How does it go on? Heavens, I've forgotten!'

> In scorching heat, in winter's icy blasts,
> We laboured with backs bent low.

She recited in a magnificent deep voice, with great feeling. Her face flushed brightly, her eyes filled with tears. This was the Varvara that used to be, Varvara the university student, and as he listened Podgorin thought of the past and recalled his student days, when he too knew much fine poetry by heart and loved to recite it.

He still has not bowed his hunched back
He's gloomily silent as before . . .

But Varvara could remember no more. She fell silent and smiled weakly, limply. After the recitation those green and red lights seemed sad.

'Oh, I've forgotten it!'

But Podgorin suddenly remembered the lines – somehow they had stuck in his memory from student days and he recited in a soft undertone,

The Russian worker has suffered enough,
In building this railway line.
He will survive to build himself
A broad bright highway
By the sweat of his brow . . .
Only the pity is . . .

'"The pity is,"' Varvara interrupted as she remembered the lines,

that neither you nor I
Will ever live to see that wonderful day.

She laughed and slapped him on the shoulder.

They went back to the house and sat down to supper. Sergey Sergeich nonchalantly stuck a corner of his serviette into his collar, imitating someone or other. 'Let's have a drink,' he said, pouring some vodka for himself and Podgorin. 'In our time, we students could hold our drink, we were fine speakers and men of action. I drink your health, old man. So why don't you drink to a stupid old idealist and wish that he will die an idealist? Can the leopard change his spots?'

Throughout supper Tatyana kept looking tenderly and jealously at her husband, anxious lest he ate or drank something that wasn't good for him. She felt that he had been spoilt by women and exhausted by them, and although this was something that appealed to her, it still distressed her. Varvara and Nadezhda also had a soft spot for him and it was obvious from the worried glances they gave him that they were scared he might suddenly get up and leave them. When he wanted to pour himself a second glass Varvara looked angry and said, 'You're poisoning yourself, Sergey Sergeich. You're a highly strung, impressionable man – you could easily become an alcoholic. Tatyana, tell him to remove that vodka.'

On the whole Sergey Sergeich had great success with women. They loved his height, his powerful build, his strong features, his idleness and his tribulations. They said that his extravagance stemmed only from extreme kindness, that he was impractical because he was an idealist. He was honest and high-principled. His inability to adapt to people or circumstances explained why he owned nothing and didn't have a steady job. They trusted him implicitly, idolized him and spoilt him with their adulation, so that he himself came to believe that he really was idealistic, impractical, honest and upright, and that he was head and shoulders above these women.

'Well, don't you have something good to say about

my little girls?' Tatyana asked as she looked lovingly at her two daughters – healthy, well-fed and like two fat buns – as she heaped rice on their plates. 'Just take a good look at them. They say all mothers can never speak ill of their children. But I do assure you I'm not at all biased. My little girls are quite remarkable. Especially the elder.'

Podgorin smiled at her and the girls and thought it strange that this healthy, young, intelligent woman, essentially such a strong and complex organism, could waste all her energy, all her strength, on such uncomplicated trivial work as running a home which was well managed anyway.

'Perhaps she knows best,' he thought. 'But it's so boring, so stupid!'

> Before he had time to groan
> A bear came and knocked him prone,

Sergey Sergeich said, snapping his fingers.

They finished their supper. Tatyana and Varvara made Podgorin sit down on a sofa in the drawing-room and, in hushed voices, talked about business again.

'We must save Sergey Sergeich,' Varvara said, 'it's our moral duty. He has his weaknesses, he's not thrifty, he doesn't put anything away for a rainy day, but that's only because he's so kind and generous. He's just a child, really. Give him a million and within a month there'd be nothing left, he'd have given it all away.'

'Yes, that's so true,' Tatyana said and tears rolled

down her cheeks. 'I've had a hard time with him, but I must admit he's a wonderful person.'

Both Tatyana and Varvara couldn't help indulging in a little cruelty, telling Podgorin reproachfully, 'Your generation, though, Misha, isn't up to much!'

'What's all this talk about generations?' Podgorin wondered. 'Surely Sergey Sergeich's no more than six years older than me?'

'Life's not easy,' Varvara sighed. 'You're always threatened with losses of some kind. First they want to take your estate away from you, or someone near and dear falls ill and you're afraid he might die. And so it goes on, day after day. But what can one do, my friends? We must submit to a Higher Power without complaining, we must remember that nothing in this world is accidental, everything has its final purpose. Now you, Misha, know little of life, you haven't suffered much and you'll laugh at me. Go ahead and laugh, but I'm going to tell you what I think. When I was passing through a stage of deepest anxiety I experienced second sight on several occasions and this completely transformed my outlook. Now I know that nothing is contingent, everything that happens in life is necessary.'

How different this Varvara was, grey-haired now, and corseted, with her fashionable long-sleeved dress – this Varvara twisting a cigarette between long, thin, trembling fingers – this Varvara so prone to mysticism – this Varvara with such a lifeless, monotonous voice. How different she was from Varvara the medical student, that cheerful, boisterous, adventurous girl with the red hair!

'Where has it all vanished to?' Podgorin wondered, bored with listening to her. 'Sing us a song, Va,' he asked to put a stop to that conversation about second sight. 'You used to have a lovely voice.'

'That's all long ago, Misha.'

'Well, recite some more Nekrasov.'

'I've forgotten it all. Those lines I recited just now I happened to remember.'

Despite the corset and long sleeves she was obviously short of money and had difficulty making ends meet at that factory beyond Tula. It was obvious she'd been overworking. That heavy, monotonous work, that perpetual interfering with other people's business and worrying about them – all this had taken its toll and had aged her. As he looked at that sad face whose freshness had faded, Podgorin concluded that in reality it was *she* who needed help, not Kuzminki or that Sergey Sergcich she was fussing about so much.

Higher education, being a doctor, didn't seem to have had any effect on the woman in her. Just like Tatyana, she loved weddings, births, christenings, interminable conversations about children. She loved spine-chilling stories with happy endings. In newspapers she only read articles about fires, floods and important ceremonies. She longed for Podgorin to propose to Nadezhda – she would have shed tears of emotion if that were to happen.

He didn't know whether it was by chance or Var-vara's doing, but Podgorin found himself alone with Nadezhda. However, the mere suspicion that he was being watched, that they wanted something from him, disturbed and inhibited him. In Nadezhda's company he felt as if they had both been put in a cage together.

'Let's go into the garden,' she said.

They went out – he feeling discontented and annoyed that he didn't know what to say, she overjoyed, proud to be near him, and obviously delighted that he was going to spend another three days with them. And perhaps she was filled with sweet fancies and hopes. He didn't know if she loved him, but he did know that she had grown used to him, that she had long been attached to him, that she considered him her teacher, that she was now experiencing the same kind of feelings as her sister Tatyana once had: all she could think of was love, of marrying as soon as possible and having a husband, children, her own place. She had still preserved that readiness for friendship which is usually so strong in children and it was highly probable that she felt for Podgorin and respected him as a friend and that she wasn't in love with *him*, but with her dreams of a husband and children.

'It's getting dark,' he said.

'Yes, the moon rises late now.'

They kept to the same path, near the house. Podgorin didn't want to go deep into the garden – it was dark there and he would have to take Nadezhda by the arm and stay very close to her. Shadows were moving on the terrace and he felt that Tatyana and Varvara were watching him.

'I must ask your advice,' Nadezhda said, stopping. 'If

Kuzminki is sold, Sergey Sergeich will leave and get a job and there's no doubt that our lives will be completely changed. I shan't go with my sister, we'll part, because I don't want to be a burden on her family. I'll take a job somewhere in Moscow. I'll earn some money and help Tatyana and her husband. You *will* give me some advice, won't you?'

Quite unaccustomed to any kind of hard work, now she was inspired at the thought of an independent, working life and making plans for the future – this was written all over her face. A life where she would be working and helping others struck her as so beautifully poetic. When he saw that pale face and dark eyebrows so close he remembered what an intelligent, keen pupil she had been, with such fine qualities, a joy to teach. Now she probably wasn't simply a young lady in search of a husband, but an intelligent, decent girl, gentle and soft-hearted, who could be moulded like wax into anything one wished. In the right surroundings she might become a truly wonderful woman!

'Well, why *don't* I marry her then?' Podgorin thought. But he immediately took fright at this idea and went off towards the house. Tatyana was sitting at the grand piano in the drawing-room and her playing conjured up bright pictures of the past, when people had played, sung and danced in that room until late at night, with the windows open and birds singing too in the garden and beyond the river. Podgorin cheered up, became play-ful, danced with Nadezhda and Varvara, and then sang. He was hampered by a corn on one foot and asked if he could wear Sergey Sergeich's slippers. Strangely, he felt at home, like one of the family, and the thought 'a typical brother-in-law' flashed through his mind. His spirits rose even higher. Looking at him the others livened up and grew cheerful, as if they had recaptured their youth. Everyone's face was radiant with hope: Kuzminki was saved! It was all so very simple in fact. They only had to think of a plan, rummage around in law books, or see that Podgorin married Nadezhda. And that little romance was going well, by all appearances. Pink, happy, her eyes brimming with tears in anticipation of something quite out of the ordinary, Nadezhda whirled round in the dance and her white dress billowed, revealing her small pretty legs in flesh-coloured stockings. Absolutely delighted, Varvara took Podgorin's arm and told him quietly and meaningly, 'Misha, don't run away from happiness. Grasp it while you can. If you wait too long you'll be running when it's too late to catch it.'

Podgorin wanted to make promises, to reassure her and even he began to believe that Kuzminki was saved – it was really so easy.

'"And thou shalt be que-een of the world",' he sang, striking a pose. But suddenly he was conscious that there was nothing he could do for these people, absolutely nothing, and he stopped singing and looked guilty.

Then he sat silently in one corner, legs tucked under him, wearing slippers belonging to someone else.

As they watched him the others understood that nothing could be done and they too fell silent. The piano was closed. Everyone noticed that it was late – it was time for bed – and Tatyana put out the large lamp in the drawing-room.

A bed was made up for Podgorin in the same little outhouse where he had stayed in the past. Sergey Sergeich went with him to wish him goodnight, holding a candle high above his head, although the moon had risen and it was bright. They walked down a path with lilac bushes on either side and the gravel crunched underfoot.

> Before he had time to groan
> A bear came and knocked him prone,

Sergey Sergeich said.

Podgorin felt that he'd heard those lines a thousand times, he was sick and tired of them! When they reached the outhouse, Sergey Sergeich drew a bottle and two glasses from his loose jacket and put them on the table.

'Brandy,' he said. 'It's a Double-O. It's impossible to have a drink in the house with Varvara around. She'd be on to me about alcoholism. But we can feel free here. It's a fine brandy.'

They sat down. The brandy was very good.

'Let's have a really good drink tonight,' Sergey Sergeich continued, nibbling a lemon. 'I've always been a gay dog myself and I like having a fling now and again. That's a *must*!'

But the look in his eyes still showed that he needed something from Podgorin and was about to ask for it.

'Drink up, old man,' he went on, sighing. 'Things are really grim at the moment. Old eccentrics like me have had their day, we're finished. Idealism's not fashionable these days. It's money that rules and if you don't want to get shoved aside you must go down on your knees and worship filthy lucre. But I can't do that, it's absolutely sickening!'

'When's the auction?' asked Podgorin, to change the subject.

'August 7th. But there's no hope at all, old man, of saving Kuzminki. There's enormous arrears and the estate doesn't bring in any income, only losses every year. It's not worth the battle. Tatyana's very cut up about it, as it's her patrimony of course. But I must admit I'm rather glad. I'm no country man. My sphere is the large, noisy city, my element's the fray!'

He kept on and on, still beating about the bush and he watched Podgorin with an eagle eye, as if waiting for the right moment.

Suddenly Podgorin saw those eyes close to him and felt his breath on his face.

'My dear fellow, please save me,' Sergey Sergeich gasped. '*Please* lend me two hundred roubles!'

Podgorin wanted to say that he was hard up too and he felt that he might do better giving two hundred roubles to some poor devil or simply losing them at cards. But he was terribly embarrassed – he felt trapped in that small room with one candle and wanted to escape as soon as possible from that breathing, from those soft arms that grasped him around the waist and which already seemed to have stuck to him like glue. Hurriedly he started feeling in his pockets for his notecase where he kept money.

'Here you are,' he muttered, taking out a hundred roubles. 'I'll give you the rest later. That's all I have on me. You see, I can't refuse.' Feeling very annoyed and beginning to lose his temper he went on. 'I'm really far too soft. Only please let me have the money back later. I'm hard up too.'

'Thank you. I'm so grateful, dear chap.'

'And please stop imagining that you're an idealist. You're as much an idealist as I'm a turkey-cock. You're simply a frivolous, indolent man, that's all.'

Sergey Sergeich sighed deeply and sat on the couch.

'My dear chap, you *are* angry,' he said. 'But if you only knew how hard things are for me! I'm going through a terrible time now. I swear it's not myself I feel sorry for, oh no! It's the wife and children. If it wasn't for my wife and children I'd have done myself in ages ago.' Suddenly his head and shoulders started shaking and he burst out sobbing.

'This really is the limit!' Podgorin said, pacing the room excitedly and feeling really furious. 'Now, what can I do with someone who has caused a great deal of harm and then starts sobbing? These tears disarm me, I'm speechless. You're sobbing, so that means you must be right.'

'Caused a great deal of harm?' Sergey Sergeich asked, rising to his feet and looking at Podgorin in amazement. 'My dear chap, what are you saying? Caused a great deal of harm? Oh, how little you know me. How little you understand me!'

'All right then, so I don't understand you, but please stop whining. It's revolting!'

'Oh, how little you know me!' Sergey Sergeich repeated, quite sincerely. 'How little!'

'Just take a look at yourself in the mirror,' Podgorin went on. 'You're no longer a young man. Soon you'll be old. It's time you stopped to think a bit and took stock of who and what you are. Spending your whole life doing nothing at all, forever indulging in empty, childish chatter, this play-acting and affectation. Doesn't it make your head go round – aren't you sick and tired of it all? Oh, it's hard going with you! You're a stupefying old bore, you are!'

With these words Podgorin left the outhouse and slammed the door. It was about the first time in his life that he had been sincere and really spoken his mind.

Shortly afterwards he was regretting having been so harsh. What was the point of talking seriously or arguing with a man who was perpetually lying, who ate and drank too much, who spent large amounts of other people's money while being quite convinced that he was an idealist and a martyr? This was a case of stupidity, or of deep-rooted bad habits that had eaten away at his organism like an illness past all cure. In any event, indignation and stern rebukes were useless in this case. Laughing at him would be more effective. One good sneer would have achieved much more than a dozen sermons!

'It's best just ignoring him,' Podgorin thought. 'Above all, not to lend him money.'

Soon afterwards he wasn't thinking about Sergey Sergeich, or about his hundred roubles. It was a calm, brooding night, very bright. Whenever Podgorin looked up at the sky on moonlit nights he had the feeling that only he and the moon were awake – everything else was either sleeping or drowsing. He gave no more thought to people or money and his mood gradually became calm and peaceful. He felt alone in this world and the sound of his own footsteps in the silence of the night seemed so mournful.

The garden was enclosed by a white stone wall. In the right-hand corner, facing the fields, stood a tower that had been built long ago, in the days of serfdom. Its lower section was of stone; the top was wooden, with a platform, a conical roof and a tall spire with a black weathercock. Down below were two gates leading straight from the garden into the fields and a staircase that creaked underfoot led up to the platform. Under the staircase some old broken armchairs had been dumped and they were bathed in the moonlight as it filtered through the gate. With their crooked upturned legs these armchairs seemed to have come to life at night and were lying in wait for someone here in the silence.

Podgorin climbed the stairs to the platform and sat down. Just beyond the fence were a boundary ditch and bank and further off were the broad fields flooded in moonlight. Podgorin knew that there was a wood exactly opposite, about two miles from the estate, and he thought that he could distinguish a dark strip in the distance. Quails and corncrakes were calling. Now and then, from the direction of the wood, came the cry of a cuckoo which couldn't sleep either.

He heard footsteps. Someone was coming across the garden towards the tower.

A dog barked.

'Beetle!' a woman's voice softly called. 'Come back, Beetle!'

He could hear someone entering the tower down below and a moment later a black dog – an old friend of Podgorin's – appeared on the bank. It stopped, looked up towards where Podgorin was sitting and wagged its tail amicably. Soon afterwards a white figure rose from the black ditch like a ghost and stopped on the bank as well. It was Nadezhda.

'Can you see something there?' she asked the dog, glancing upwards.

She didn't see Podgorin but probably sensed that he was near, since she was smiling and her pale, moonlit face was happy. The tower's black shadow stretching over the earth, far into the fields, that motionless white figure with the blissfully smiling, pale face, the black dog and both their shadows – all this was just like a dream.

'Someone *is* there,' Nadezhda said softly.

She stood waiting for him to come down or to call her up to him, so that he could at last declare his love – then both would be happy on that calm, beautiful night. White, pale, slender, very lovely in the moonlight, she awaited his caresses. She was weary of perpetually dreaming of love and happiness and was unable to conceal her feelings any longer. Her whole figure, her radiant eyes, her fixed happy smile, betrayed her innermost thoughts. But he felt awkward, shrank back and didn't make a sound, not knowing whether to speak, whether to make the habitual joke out of the situation or whether to remain silent. He felt annoyed and his only thought was that here, in a country garden on a moonlit night, close to a beautiful, loving, thoughtful girl, he felt the same apathy as on Little Bronny Street: evidently this type of romantic situation had lost its fascination, like *that* prosaic depravity. Of no consequence to him now were those meetings on moonlit nights, those white shapes with slim waists, those mysterious shadows, towers, country estates and characters such as Sergey Sergeich, and people like himself, Podgorin, with his icy indifference, his constant irritability, his inability to adapt to reality and take what it had to offer, his wearisome, obsessive craving for what did not and never could exist on earth. And now, as he sat in that tower, he would have preferred a good fireworks display, or some moonlight procession, or Varvara reciting Nekrasov's *The Railway* again. He would rather another woman was standing there on the bank where Nadezhda was: this other woman would have told him something absolutely fascinating and new that had nothing to do with love or happiness. And if she did happen to speak of love, this would have been a summons to those new, lofty, rational aspects of existence on whose threshold we are perhaps already living and of which we sometimes seem to have premonitions.

'There's no one there,' Nadezhda said.

She stood there for another minute or so, then she walked quietly towards the wood, her head bowed. The dog ran on ahead. Podgorin could see her white figure for quite a long time. 'To think how it's all turned out, though . . .' he repeated to himself as he went back to the outhouse.

He had no idea what he could say to Sergey Sergeich or Tatyana the next day or the day after that, or how he would treat Nadezhda. And he felt embarrassed, frightened and bored in advance. How was he going to fill those three long days which he had promised to spend here? He remembered the conversation about second sight and Sergey Sergeich quoting the lines:

Before he had time to groan
A bear came and knocked him prone.

He remembered that tomorrow, to please Tatyana, he would have to smile at those well-fed, chubby little girls – and he decided to leave.

At half past five in the morning Sergey Sergeich appeared on the terrace of the main house in his Bokhara dressing-gown and tasselled fez. Not losing a moment, Podgorin went over to him to say goodbye.

'I have to be in Moscow by ten,' he said, looking away. 'I'd completely forgotten I'm expected at the Notary Public's office. Please excuse me. When the others are up please tell them that I apologize. I'm dreadfully sorry.'

In his hurry he didn't hear Sergey Sergeich's answer and he kept looking round at the windows of the big house, afraid that the ladies might wake up and stop him going. He was ashamed he felt so nervous. He sensed that this was his last visit to Kuzminki, that he would never come back. As he drove away he glanced back several times at the outhouse where once he had spent so many happy days. But deep down he felt coldly indifferent, not at all sad.

At home the first thing he saw on the table was the note he'd received the day before: 'Dear Misha,' he read. 'You've completely forgotten us, please come and visit us soon.' And for some reason he remembered Nadezhda whirling round in the dance, her dress billowing, revealing her legs in their flesh-coloured stockings . . .

Ten minutes later he was at his desk working – and he didn't give Kuzminki another thought.

POCKET PENGUINS

POCKET PENGUINS